W

Bunjitsu Bunny
vs.
Bunjitsu Bunny

Bunjitsu Bunny
vs.
Bunjitsu Bunny

Written and illustrated by
John Himmelman

Henry Holt and Company
New York

For Sifu Sean Gallimore,
who taught me much!

Henry Holt and Company, *Publishers since 1866*
Henry Holt® is a registered trademark of Macmillan Publishing Group, LLC.
175 Fifth Avenue, New York, New York 10010 · mackids.com

Library of Congress Cataloging-in-Publication Data
Names: Himmelman, John, author, illustrator.
Title: Bunjitsu Bunny vs. Bunjitsu Bunny / written and illustrated by John Himmelman.
Other titles: Bunjitsu Bunny versus Bunjitsu Bunny
Description: First edition. | New York : Henry Holt and Company, 2017. |
Sequel to: Bunjitsu Bunny jumps the moon | Summary: Follow Isabel, the best bunjitsu artist in
her school, as she makes friends, faces her fears, and fights her toughest opponent yet—herself.
Identifiers: LCCN 2017022329 (print) | LCCN 2016050391 (ebook) |
ISBN 9781627797337 (hardcover) | ISBN 9781250139764 (ebook)
Subjects: | CYAC: Martial arts—Fiction. | Rabbits—Fiction. | Animals—Fiction.
Classification: LCC PZ7.H5686 (print) | LCC PZ7.H5686 Brv 2017 (ebook) | DDC [Fic]—dc23
LC record available at https://lccn.loc.gov/2017022329

Our books may be purchased in bulk for promotional, educational, or business use.
Please contact your local bookseller or the Macmillan Corporate and Premium Sales Department
at (800) 221-7945 ext. 5442 or by e-mail at MacmillanSpecialMarkets@macmillan.com.

First edition—2017
Printed in China by RR Donnelley Asia Printing Solutions Ltd.,
Dongguan City, Guangdong Province

1 3 5 7 9 10 8 6 4 2

Contents

Isabel

Isabel was the best bunjitsu artist in her school. She could kick higher than anyone. She could hit harder than anyone. She could throw her classmates farther than anyone.

Some were frightened of her. But Isabel never hurt another creature, unless she had to.

"Bunjitsu is not just about kicking, hitting, and throwing," she said. "It is about finding ways NOT to kick, hit, and throw."

They called her Bunjitsu Bunny.

Listen

"A bunny can travel for miles while sitting in one spot," said Teacher to his bunjitsu students.

"That is impossible," said Kyle.

"No," said Teacher. "You can travel with your ears. I want you all to go sit in the woods and listen. How far can you *hear*?"

The bunnies did as Teacher asked.

"All I hear are breathing bunnies," whispered Kyle.

"I hear Ben's tapping foot," said Wendy.

"I hear the breeze in the leaves," said Ben.

"What do you hear?" Ben asked
Isabel.

Isabel listened. "I hear Sparrow by
the river."

She listened harder. "I hear Woodpecker far across the lake."

She listened even harder. "Dolphin just splashed in the ocean!"

"Keep going!" said her friends.

"I hear Elephant calling her baby.

"I hear Panda munching on bamboo.

"I hear Penguin burp!" She giggled.

"Keep going! Keep going!" said
the bunnies.

Isabel listened as hard as she could.

"I hear Mountain Goat's hooves on the rocks.

"I hear Crow sneezing.

"I hear . . . Max scratching his nose!"

"That's because I'm right next to you," said Max.

"But I heard you from there," said Isabel. She pointed in the direction opposite Max.

"You heard me from all the way around the world!" said Max.

"Wow," said Isabel. "Teacher was right again. He is a very wise rabbit!"

Back at the school, Teacher
smiled. "Why, thank you, Isabel,"
he said.

Bunjitsu Bunny vs. Bunjitsu Bunny

Isabel won match after match at the bunjitsu tournament.

"No one can beat Bunjitsu Bunny," said Ben.

"That is not true," said Isabel.

"Isabel is right," said Wendy. "I know someone who can beat her. You will see in class tomorrow."

The next day, Wendy entered the school. She was alone.

"Where is the challenger?" asked Ben.

"She is standing in front of me," said Wendy. "The only one who can beat Bunjitsu Bunny is Bunjitsu Bunny."

Isabel laughed. "You want me to fight myself?"

"If you think you can win," said Wendy.

Isabel laughed again. "Okay, here goes."

Bunjitsu Bunny threw a lightning-fast paw to her face. Bunjitsu Bunny ducked.

Bunjitsu Bunny grabbed her shoulder for a rabbit flip. Bunjitsu Bunny twisted her paw. "Ow, ow, ow!" she said.

Bunjitsu Bunny pulled up her legs and slammed to the ground. Bunjitsu Bunny rolled over and got away.

"Do you give up?" she asked herself.

"Never!" she answered.

The bunny fought herself back and forth across the school. It was the toughest battle anyone had ever seen!

In the end, she was too tired to move.

"I think it was a tie," said Wendy.

"I don't know," said Ben. "I think Bunjitsu Bunny won."

Isabel stood up. She shook her own paw and said, "That was a good fight. I hope I never have to go against you again!"

"Me too," she answered.

Carrot Contest

The bunnies entered the big carrot-growing contest.

Soon the leaves of Kyle's carrots were up to his knees.

The leaves of Betsy's carrots were up to her thighs.

The leaves of Max's carrots were up to his waist!

Isabel watered her carrots every day, but nothing seemed to be growing.

"It is a waste of time," said Max. "You are just watering dirt."

"We'll see," said Isabel.

Summer arrived. The carrot contest was just two weeks away.

The leaves of Kyle's carrots were up to his waist.

The leaves of Betsy's carrots were up to her chest.

The leaves of Max's carrots were up to his chin!

Isabel's single carrot leaf reached no higher than her toe.

"It's time to give up," said Kyle.

"We'll see," said Isabel.

On the morning of the contest, they all picked their largest carrot.

Isabel waited to pull hers.

"I don't think there is a carrot under there," said Kyle.

"We'll see," said Isabel. "Just a little bit longer . . ."

Everyone's carrots were lined up for judging.

"Kyle's carrot is the biggest," said the judge. Then he looked at Betsy's carrot.

"Wait a minute. Betsy's carrot is a little bigger!" Then he looked at Max's carrot.

"Hold on now. Max's carrot is even bigger!"

Isabel plopped her carrot on the table. It was bigger than she was!

"And the winning carrot belongs to Isabel!" said the judge.

"Did you know it would be so big?" asked Kyle.

"No," said Isabel. "But I knew it would *not* be if I gave up."

Rolling Race

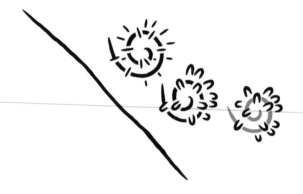

Isabel and Max met Porcupine.

"Hello, Bunjitsu Bunny," said Porcupine.

"Hello," said Isabel.

"Hello, Bunjitsu Bunny's brother," added Porcupine.

"I'm Max," said Max.

"Everyone just calls you Bunjitsu Bunny's brother," said Porcupine.

"No," said Isabel. "Everyone calls him Max."

"Are you better at bunjitsu than your sister?" asked Porcupine.

"No," said Max.

"Are you smarter than your sister?" asked Porcupine.

"Sometimes," said Max.

"Are you faster than your sister?" asked Porcupine.

"I am faster than *you*," said Max.

"I am faster than both of you," said Porcupine. Porcupine pointed to the top of a very tall hill. "Let's have a rolling race down that hill."

"That's pretty steep," Max
whispered to Isabel.

"I know," Isabel whispered back.

The three climbed to the top of
the hill.

"Ready, set, GO!" shouted
Porcupine. They rolled down the
hill. First Isabel was winning. Then
Porcupine was winning. Then Max
was winning. Then Max hit a bush.

"GO, ISABEL!" cheered Max.

"I CAN'T STOP!" shouted Isabel.

"I CAN'T STOP, EITHER!"
shouted Porcupine.

Max ran down the hill. He tackled
his sister.

"Thank you, Max," she said. "I was
getting dizzy!"

Porcupine rolled past them.
"HELP!" he called.

Max chased after him. "Your tail
is too pointy! I can't grab it," he
said.

Max had an idea. He rolled
down the hill and zipped right past
Porcupine. The rabbit curled up in a
ball. Porcupine rolled over him and
shot into the air. He stuck to a tree.

"What do you think of 'Bunjitsu Bunny's brother' now?" asked Isabel.

"His name is Max," said Porcupine.

Isabel smiled. "And you can call me 'Max's sister.'"

Falling Leaves

Teacher stared out the window. "Look at all those leaves. Would any of you like to help out our school by raking them up?"

Nobody liked raking leaves, but Isabel raised her paw.

"Blah," said Ben. "I will, too, I guess."

"Ugh," moaned Betsy. "I guess I will also."

"I guess so," said Kyle. "But *blah* and *ugh,* too."

The bunnies went outside and raked the leaves.

"I heard that it is good luck to catch a leaf before it lands on the ground," said Betsy.

They dropped their rakes and waited for a leaf to fall. Soon one did, and Isabel dove to catch it before it landed.

Another leaf broke loose. "I've got it!" yelled Betsy, and she caught it.

"Watch what I do with the next one," said Ben. He caught it on his nose.

Another leaf fell. Kyle kicked it into the air and grabbed it with his teeth. Everyone clapped.

The bunnies spent the rest of the
day catching leaves. Soon they all
had big armloads of them.

Isabel dumped her leaves on top
of the bigger pile they had raked
earlier.

"Now you won't have good luck!" cried Kyle.

"No," said Isabel. "They are not on the ground. They are on a pile of leaves!"

They all added their leaves to the pile.

"So where is the good luck?" asked Kyle.

Isabel looked at her friends and smiled.

"YEEEEAAAA!" she shouted as she ran and jumped in the pile. The other bunnies joined her.

"Is it good luck to have fun?"
asked Betsy.

"I feel pretty lucky," said Isabel,
and she dove back into the leaves.

Shooting Star

Three bunnies sat looking up at the night sky. Isabel joined them.

"We are looking for a shooting star," said Max. "If you make a wish when you see one, it comes true."

A shooting star flashed overhead.

"I wish for a blueberry pie," said Ben.

"I wish for new bunchucks," said Wendy.

"I wish I didn't have to clean my room," said Max. "What do you wish for, Isabel?"

Isabel smiled and walked away.

The next morning, Ben found a big, warm blueberry pie waiting for him.

"My wish came true!" he said.

"I am so happy for you," said Isabel.

"Did your wish come true?" asked Ben.

"Not yet," said Isabel.

Later that day, Wendy found a
new pair of bunchucks next to her
old ones.

"My wish came true!" she screamed.

"I am so happy for you," said
Isabel.

"Did your wish come true?" asked
Wendy.

"Almost," said Isabel.

That evening, Max went into his room. It was cleaner than it had ever been.

"My wish came true!" he shouted.

"I am so happy for you," said Isabel.

"Did your wish come true?" asked Max.

"It did!" said Isabel, and she left the room.

Later that night, the four bunnies
met beneath the stars again.

"Our wishes came true," said Ben.
"But I think Isabel had something
to do with it. Did you bake me that
blueberry pie?"

Isabel blushed. "Yes," she said.

"Wait," said Wendy. "Did you make me those new bunchucks?"

"Yes," said Isabel.

"And I guess you cleaned my room," said Max.

"Yes," said Isabel.

"Will you tell us what your wish was?" asked Ben.

"I wished my friends' wishes would come true," she said.

"But you made them come true," said Wendy.

"It is easy to make wishes," said Isabel. "It is more fun to make them come true."

Little Footprints

Challenge Bunjitsu Bunny

"Look what someone wrote in the dirt," said Wendy. "It says, 'I challenge Bunjitsu Bunny.'"

"Who wrote that?" asked Isabel.

"I don't know," said Kyle. "Why does everyone want to challenge you?"

"Because," said Wendy, "Bunjitsu Bunny is the best. If you beat her, *you* become the best."

"That is just silly," said Isabel.

"Look at those footprints," said Kyle. "Whoever wrote this message is tiny."

The footprints led to a cave in the woods.

"I will deal with this little troublemaker," said Wendy. She went into the cave.

CRASH! SLAM! BOOM!

Wendy flew out of the cave.

"Leave it to me," said Kyle. He
went into the cave.

BOOM! SLAM! CRASH!

Kyle flew out of the cave.

"Go get him, Isabel," said Wendy.

"No," said Isabel. "I have no reason to fight—" Then Isabel was yanked inside.

SLAM! CRASH! BOOM!

Isabel flew out of the cave.

"Now I have a reason," she said, and ran back in.

SLAM! CRASH! BOOM! BOOM! CRASH! SLAM!

Out rolled Isabel and a little
weevil. They fought back and forth.
It was a battle like no one had seen
before. Isabel finally held him down.

"Stop fighting," she said.

The weevil stood and bowed.

"I am Weejitsu Weevil," he said. "I admit defeat."

"Why did you want to fight me?" asked Isabel.

"Because if I could defeat the great Bunjitsu Bunny, then Weejitsu Weevil would be the best in the forest."

"Fighting for no reason does not make you the best," said Isabel. "It makes you a bully."

"You are right," said the weevil. "I see why you are the best. Thank you for the lesson."

The bunnies walked back home. They saw the little footprints that had led them to the weevil.

"That's funny," said Kyle. "Those footprints don't look so small anymore."

Invisible Bunny

Isabel went for a walk.

"Hello, Bunjitsu Bunny," said a voice.

"Who said that?" asked Isabel.

"I did," said the voice.

Isabel looked around her. "Are you invisible?" she asked.

"No," the voice said, laughing. "I'm right in front of you."

"Oh, hi, Katydid!" said Isabel. "How do you make yourself so hard to see?"

"I look like a leaf," said Katydid. "If I stay near leaves, I am almost invisible."

"I would like to be invisible," said Isabel. "I will hide, and you try to find me."

Isabel stuck leaves in her fur and hid in a bush. "Come and find me," she called.

"I see you, Bunjitsu Bunny," said Katydid. "You still look like a bunny."

"I will try again," said Isabel. She rolled in mud and lay down in a mud puddle. "Come and find me," she called.

"I see you, Bunjitsu Bunny," said Katydid. "You still look like a bunny."

Maybe I can hide in the water, thought Isabel.

"Come and find me," she called.

"Hmmm," said Katydid. "I don't see Bunjitsu Bunny, but I do see her ears."

"I know. I still look like a bunny,"
said Isabel.

"I guess bunnies can't be invisible,"
said Katydid.

"You don't know this one very
well," said Isabel.

Isabel hopped off. Katydid waited
for her to call. She grew tired of waiting
and set out to find Bunjitsu Bunny.

She saw some bunnies in the
meadow but did not see Isabel. "Have
you seen Bunjitsu Bunny?" she asked.

Isabel stepped forward. "Here I am!" she said.

"You changed your clothes! I did not know that was you!" said Katydid.

Isabel laughed. "That is because I still look like a bunny."

The Wind

"It is a very windy day today," said Teacher. "A good bunjitsu student can stand against the strongest winds."

"Even on Hurricane Hill?" asked Kyle.

"Yes," said Teacher. "Even on Hurricane Hill."

The bunnies rushed to the hill.
It was so windy, they could hardly
stand up.

Kyle pounded his chest. "No wind can push me down," he said. He crawled to the top of the hill and stood up to face the wind. Wendy grabbed him just before he blew away.

"I know the secret," said Wendy. She picked up a heavy rock and climbed to the top of the hill. "I'm doing it!" she shouted.

But the rock grew heavy, and she
put it down. The wind picked up her
feet. Wendy held on to the rock.

"Help!" she called. Ben pulled her
down.

"I will do this," said Ben. "Kyle, get behind me and push." Ben and Kyle inched up to the top of the hill. The wind inched them back down.

"My turn," said Isabel. She climbed the hill.

"I will push you back!" she said,
and pushed the wind with her paws.
The wind pushed *her* back. Then
she turned her paws sideways. The
wind stopped pushing and went right
around them.

Isabel stood there, up on the hill, and turned her body sideways. The wind whistled past her.

She climbed down to join her friends.

"How did you keep from being blown down?" asked Kyle.

"I think sometimes it's easier to let something go by you than it is to stop it," said Isabel.

Flying Kites

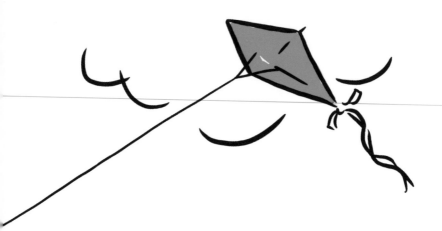

It was a beautiful, breezy day.

"Let's make kites and fly them," said Isabel. Everyone went home to make their kites, then returned to the meadow.

Isabel's kite looked like a big diamond.

Wendy's kite looked like a little diamond.

Ben's kite looked like a bat.

"Where is Max?" asked Wendy.

"Here I am," said a voice under a giant kite.

"Isn't that a little big?" asked Isabel.

"The bigger the better," said Max.

They launched their kites into the air. Isabel's kite danced in big circles. Wendy's kite danced in little circles. Ben's kite darted back and forth.

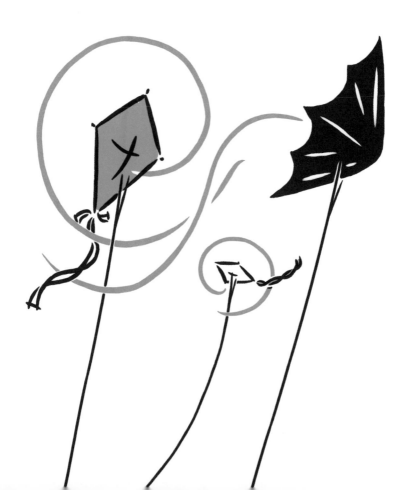

Max's kite went WHOOMPH and
lifted him into the air!
"HELP!" he called.

"Don't let go," shouted Isabel. She
raced up a tree to grab her brother.
He sailed by, right above her.

"HEEELP!" shouted Max.

Isabel had an idea.

"Quickly," she said to the others, "hand me the strings to your kites." Isabel grabbed the strings. The kites lifted her into the air.

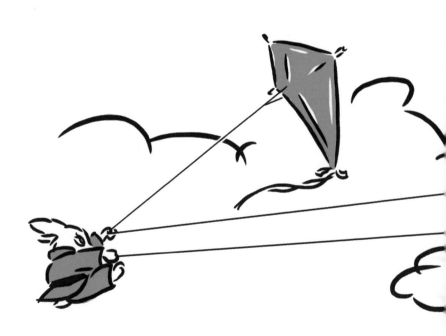

Isabel's big diamond kite carried her high. Wendy's little diamond kite pulled her fast. Ben's bat kite steered her back and forth.

She soon caught up to Max.

"Got you!" she said.

Isabel let go of her kite, and they dropped a little lower. Then she let go of Wendy's kite, and they slowed down. When she let go of Ben's kite, she and Max floated to the ground.

"That was way too scary!" said Max, and he went home.

"There's still a good breeze," said Ben. "Let's go fly our kites!"

Isabel's kite danced in big circles.
Wendy's kite danced in little circles.
Ben's kite darted back and forth.
Max arrived with his new kite. It was
so small, they could hardly see it.

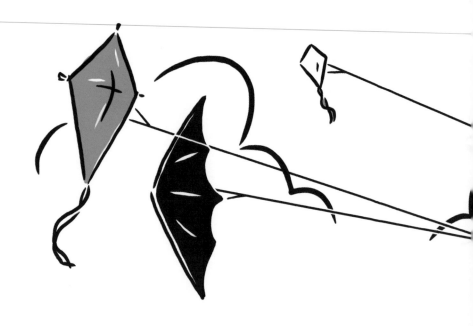

"I'm not taking any chances," he said. They spent the rest of the day with kites in the air and feet on the ground.

Bunjitsu Bunny vs. the Germs

Isabel had a bad cold. Her nose was stuffy. Her throat was scratchy. Betsy brought some warm soup to help her feel better.

"Colds are caused by germs in your body," said Betsy. "When they are gone, you will feel better."

"I wish I was small enough to chase them out," said Isabel.

Betsy laughed. "If anyone could, Bunjitsu Bunny could," she said, and went home.

Isabel fell asleep. She dreamed she was a tiny Bunjitsu Bunny. In front of her was an army of germs.

"Okay, germs," she said. "It is time to leave."

"We like it here," said the germs.

Tiny Bunjitsu Bunny kicked the germs. Her feet bounced right off them.

"Ha, ha, ha!" laughed the germs. "Bunjitsu Bunny is tickling us!"

Tiny Bunjitsu Bunny pounded the germs with mighty bunjitsu punches. Her fists bounced right off them.

"Hee, hee, hee!" laughed the germs. "More tickles from Bunjitsu Bunny."

Tiny Bunjitsu Bunny leapt onto the
germs. She bounced right off them.

"Ho, ho, ho!" laughed the germs.
"It's a bouncing Bunjitsu Bunny!"

Maybe hitting fast and hard is not the answer, thought Tiny Bunjitsu Bunny. She walked slowly up to a germ and gently placed her paws on it. Then she gave it a push. The germ fell backward!

"AHA!" she said.

She pushed and pushed the germs.
They could not stop her. She saw light
up ahead and pushed them toward it.

"NOOOOOO!" cried the germs.

"OUT!" shouted Tiny Isabel.

Suddenly Big Isabel sneezed. She opened her eyes and sat up. Her nose was no longer stuffy. Her throat was no longer scratchy. The germs were gone!

Bunjitsu Bunny shook her fist in the air. "And STAY out!" she said.

108

Snowy Owl

A big snowstorm came in the night. The next morning, Isabel saw an owl in the distance.

"Are you okay?" she asked.

The owl opened her eyes. "I am Snowy Owl," she said. "I live in the far, far north, but I got lost in the storm. I am so worried about my family, but I am too tired to fly home."

Isabel thought a moment. "How long did it take you to fly here?" she asked.

"Two days and a night," said Snowy.

"Hmmm. Then it should take a week to walk," said Isabel.

"I can't walk, either," said Snowy.

"But I can," said Isabel. "I will be right back."

Isabel returned with her sled. She helped Snowy aboard and began her journey. For two days, Isabel

marched through the frosty meadow.
Snowy Owl slept. At night, Isabel
made a shelter out of snow. Isabel
slept. Snowy slept some more.

On days three and four, Isabel pulled Snowy through a wintry forest and across a frozen lake. Snowy Owl slept. At night, Isabel made a shelter out of snow. Isabel slept. Snowy slept some more.

On days five and six, Isabel
pushed through a snow-filled valley
and crossed an icy bridge. Snowy
Owl slept. At night, Isabel made
a shelter out of snow. Isabel slept.
Snowy slept some more.

On day seven, they crossed snow-covered mountains. Isabel pulled Snowy up the hills and rode with her down the hills. She was too tired to enjoy the ride. At night, she made a shelter out of snow. Isabel slept and slept and slept. Snowy flew off.

Isabel woke up in the evening.

Four owl faces looked down at her.

"You found your family!" she said.

"Thanks to you!" said Snowy.

"And now we will take you home."

The owls helped Isabel onto her sled and carried her through the winter sky. Isabel slept the whole way.